D1254463

This book belongs to

Kate

First paperback edition 1996

First published 1989 in hardback by
A & C Black (Publishers) Limited
35 Bedford Row, London WC1R 4JH

ISBN 0–7136–4410–9

Text copyright © 1996, 1989 Sue Brearley
Photographs copyright © 1996, 1989 Jenny Matthews

A CIP catalogue record for this book
is available from the British Library.

All rights reserved. No part of this publication may be
reproduced or used in any form or by any means –
photographic, electronic or mechanical, including
photocopying, recording, taping or information storage and
retrieval systems – without written permission of the
publishers.

Filmset by August Filmsetting, Haydock, St Helens
Printed in Belgium by Proost International Book Production

Talk to me

Sue Brearley

Photographs by Jenny Matthews

A & C Black · London

Everybody wants to talk to their friends.
Talking is a way of sharing how you feel.

Little children learn to speak by listening to other people. Sometimes they copy what they hear. They try out different words and sounds.

Not everyone starts to speak at the same age, in the same way. Some children take longer than others.

Some children have problems with speaking clearly.
Some children can't speak at all.
If you can't speak, you have to find
a different way of talking.

If you are deaf, it's hard to understand what
different sounds mean. You might be able to
hear someone banging a drum, or feel the
vibrations from a musical instrument. But
hearing what people say to you is more
difficult.

If you can't hear what people say, you can't copy the words they use. It is very hard for deaf children to learn to speak. Deaf people have to lipread.

They watch people's lips to see what each person is saying.

'oo'

'f'

'th'

Some deaf people talk with their hands.
They use sign language to share how they feel.

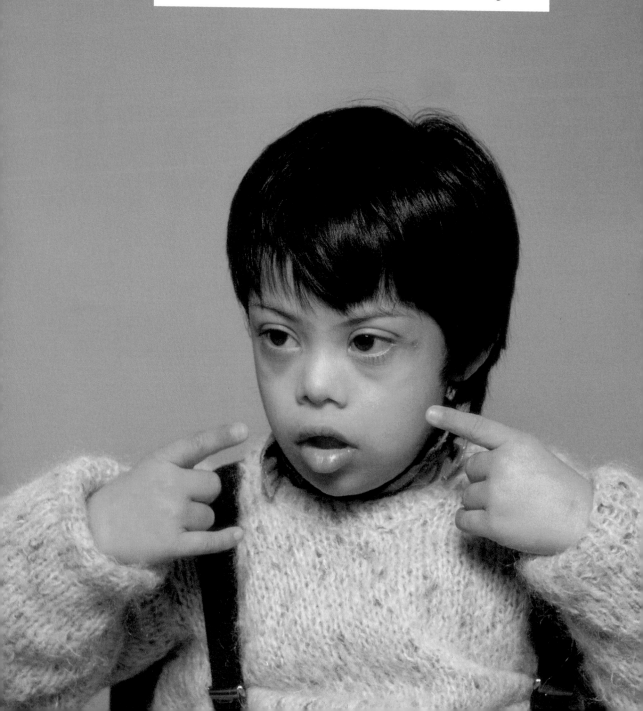

For people who are deaf and blind, there is another kind of sign language. Children have to learn to feel the different signs with their hands.

Some children can't speak because they are disabled. Imagine that you wanted to say something, but you couldn't move your tongue or your lips properly. The words you made might sound strange – or perhaps you couldn't make words at all.

If you had a disability like this, you could hear
what people said to you, and you could
understand them. But other people couldn't
always understand you. Perhaps you couldn't
use sign language because your hands didn't
work properly either.

Children who find speaking difficult can go to a speech therapist. Some children who go to a therapist are disabled, or can't hear very well. But lots of other children may need speech therapy at some time in their lives.

The speech therapist
helps people to
practise making
different sounds, and
to work at the difficult
words. They can learn
to move their lips and
tongue so that the
words come out more
clearly.

Playing a game can
sometimes help too.
This computer makes
sounds and pictures
when you use the right
words.

These children can talk by pointing to little pictures on a board or in a book. The pictures are called symbols and each one has a meaning. The symbols are the same whatever language you speak, so people from different countries can use them to talk to each other.

Some of the children use their hands to point with, and some use their feet. Children who can't use their hands or feet can look at the symbol they want. The person they are talking to has to work out which symbol they are looking at. It takes longer than speaking or using sign language, but they can share how they feel.

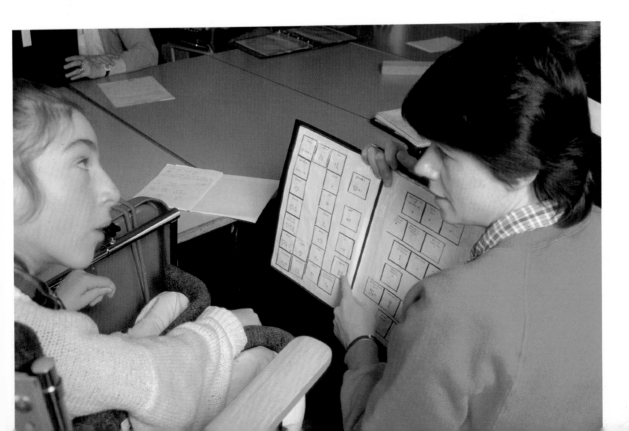

Some children learn things slowly. It can be
hard work learning how to walk, and how to eat
and drink by yourself. Learning to speak can be
hard work too, and sometimes it takes a long time.

Sometimes children who learn slowly talk with sign language. Sometimes they speak and use sign language at the same time. It can make things easier when they want to talk. They might need to ask for something. Or perhaps they want to talk about what they have been doing – like building a sand castle.

Some children get mixed up about what they want to say. When they speak, they might use the wrong words or say the wrong thing. People might not understand what they mean.

It's upsetting when this happens,
especially if other people laugh or get cross.
It makes it hard to share how you feel,
and hard to make new friends.

Children who can't
speak can find ways to
talk. But you can't
talk if other people
don't talk to you. You
can't share your
feelings if other people
don't listen to you.

Do you know someone who doesn't speak?
If you do, she probably wants to talk to you.
Are you letting her talk?
Do you know how she talks?

She might lipread

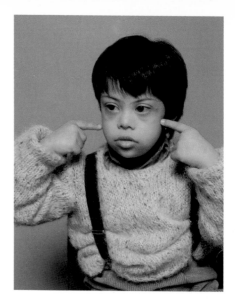

She might use sign language

She might use symbols

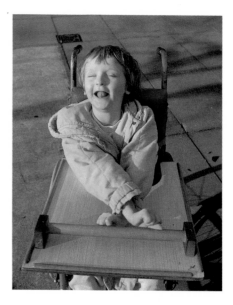

She might just need you to wait and listen while she works out what she wants to say.

Does someone want to talk to you?

More about different ways of talking.

You might like to learn the "finger alphabet" – it's a good way of talking privately to your friends, and it doesn't take long.

If you would like to know more about different kinds of sign language, here are some addresses you can write to:

National Deaf Children's Society
45 Hereford Road
London W2 5AH

The Association for all Speech Impaired children
347 Central Market
Smithfield
London EC1A 9NH

In Australia:
The Deaf Council
340 Highett Road
Victoria 3190

In New Zealand:
The New Zealand Association of the Deaf
P.O. Box 408
Auckland 1

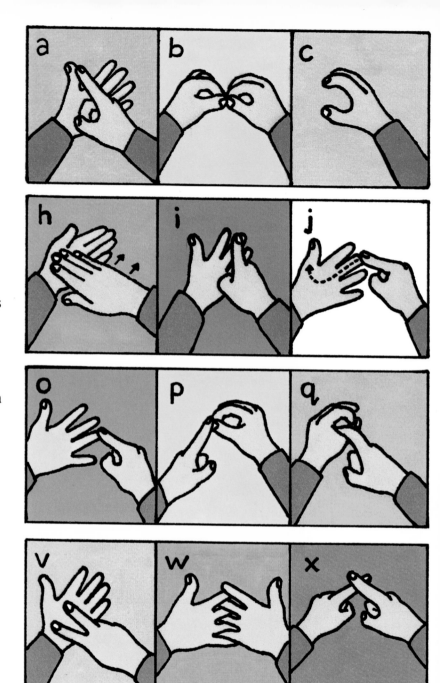

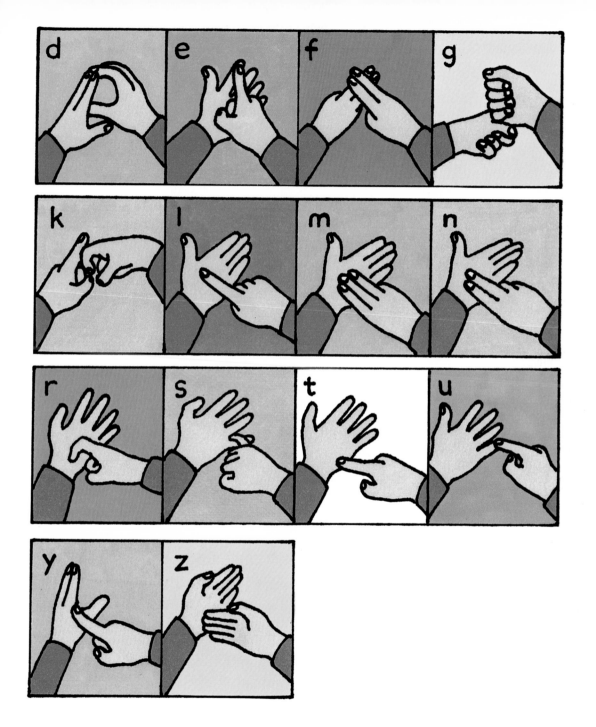

25